ENDANGERED!

ZEBRAS

Shona Grimbly

Series Consultant: James G. Doherty
General Curator, The Bronx Zoo, New York

BENCHMARK BOOKS

MARSHALL CAVENDISH
NEW YORK

Benchmark Books
Marshall Cavendish Corporation
99 White Plains Road
Tarrytown, New York 10591-9001

Library of Congress Cataloging-in-Publication Data

Grimbly, Shona
   Zebras / Shona Grimbly.
      p. cm. — (Endangered!)
   Includes bibliographic references (p.   ) and index.
   Summary: Describes the physical characteristics, habits, and natural environment of the last
three species of zebras left in the world—the plains zebra, the mountain zebra, and Grevy's
zebra. Also discusses what is being done to protect these animals from complete extinction.
   ISBN 0-7614-0320-5 (lib. bdg.)
   1. Zebras—Juvenile literature. 2. Endangered species—Juvenile
literature. [1. Zebras. 2. Endangered species.] I. Title.
II. Series.
QL737.U62G755 1999
599.665'7—dc21

                                                98-14507
                                                 CIP
                                                   AC

Printed in Hong Kong

PICTURE CREDITS
*The publishers would like to thank the Natural History Photographic Agency (NHPA) for
supplying all the photographs used in this book except for the following: 11, 12, 24, 25, 26,
27 Corbis UK Ltd.*

Series created by Brown Packaging

Front cover: Plains zebras.
Title page: Zebras at water hole.
Back cover: Zebras fighting.

Contents

Introduction

Most of us have seen pictures of zebras in books or on television. With their black and white stripes, zebras look like painted horses. In fact, zebras are related to horses and donkeys. Like horses, they have long, thin legs to help them run fast. Their teeth are strong and designed for eating grass. Zebras have a bushy mane on the top of their neck. Their tail has a tuft at the end, which is useful for brushing off flies and mosquitoes. Zebras are smaller than horses. Their striped coats make them instantly recognizable.

Zebras live in Africa, mostly in the tropical grasslands of east Africa. Three hundred years ago, great herds of zebras roamed all over South Africa. These zebras were called

This group of plains zebras is keeping a careful watch for any enemies. Zebras look like stocky horses with painted stripes.

quaggas by the local people. European settlers in South Africa in the 1700s hunted and killed these zebras for food. By 1900, the quaggas of South Africa had become **extinct**.

Today, there are only three **species** of zebra left. The most common is the plains zebra. Plains zebras live in eastern and southern Africa. They range from south-east Sudan to South Africa and Angola. Plains zebras measure about 50 inches (130 cm) from the ground to their shoulders. The plains zebra is not threatened with extinction, but the numbers have dropped in recent years.

The second species is the mountain zebra. This species lives on high grasslands and plateaus in southwest Africa. Mountain zebras are smaller than plains zebras and more

Zebras live on the grasslands and plains of Africa.

AFRICA

- Grevy's Zebra
- Mountain Zebra
- Plains Zebra

Areas where
zebras live

agile. They are about 47 inches (120 cm) tall. They have narrow hoofs to help them pick their way along rocky slopes. There are two types, or **subspecies**, of mountain zebra. These are the Cape mountain zebra and the Hartmann's zebra. Both types are becoming very rare.

The Cape mountain zebra almost died out completely in 1913. The number of animals had dropped to just 27 before they were put into the Mountain Zebra National Park in Cape Province in South Africa to protect them. Hartmann's zebra is also in danger of dying out. There are about 7,000 animals living in Namibia, which is in southwest Africa. Very few live anywhere else.

Mountain zebras are very agile. They have hard hoofs. This helps them pick their way up and down rocky slopes.

The third species of zebra is Grevy's zebra. This was named after Jules Grevy (1801–1891), who was president of France. The emperor of Ethiopia gave him a zebra as a present. Grevy's zebra is the largest zebra of them all, measuring up to 63 inches (160 cm) tall. It is much heavier than the plains and mountain zebras, too. Grevy's zebra has very big ears and a long narrow head, making it look a lot like a donkey.

The Grevy's zebra has an attractive coat with closely spaced narrow stripes. Sadly, hunters have killed these zebras for their skins. There are no more than 4,000 or so of these beautiful animals surviving now, in protected areas of Ethiopia and northern Kenya.

With their big ears and long heads, Grevy's zebras look like donkeys. They make a noise like a donkey, too.

Plains zebras are very sociable. They live in small family groups.

How Zebras Live

The plains zebras and the mountain zebras live in family groups called **harems**. Each harem has a head **stallion** (male zebra) as the leader. The stallion has several **mares** (females), and each mare has two or three young with her. Plains zebras usually live in groups of up to 16 animals. A mountain zebra harem has from 5 to 12 members.

The family group roams over the grasslands eating whatever **forage** can be found. Zebras need to eat a great deal, so they graze almost continuously. When the herd has eaten all the grass in one area, it moves on to find more food somewhere else.

The head stallion looks after his family and will fight off another stallion who tries to steal away or **mate** with one of his mares. Young zebras stay with their mothers for several years. Stallions leave the family group of their own accord when they are about two to three years old. They join a **bachelor group** with other young stallions. The young bachelor zebras live together until they are fully adult, at about five to six years. Then they leave the group to find a mare to mate with and form their own family.

The young females may leave the group to mate with another stallion or they may stay with the family and mate with the head stallion.

Zebras need good grazing ground and water to survive. The herd is constantly on the move, seeking new food

Two young zebras from the same family group. The mare on the left is probably the mother of one of the foals.

supplies as it eats up all the grass on the old ground. The grazing ground must also be near a water hole, where the herd goes to drink at night. When a herd or family group is grazing or drinking at a water hole, one member of the family—usually a young stallion—is "put on guard" to watch out for danger.

Strangely enough, when the herd moves off to a new pasture, it is not the head stallion that leads the way but the senior mare with her **foals**. She is followed by the other mares, each with her own foals. The mares always follow in the same order. Each mare knows her place and keeps to it whenever the herd is on the move. The stallion walks behind or along the side to protect his family from enemies.

This family group is enjoying a cool drink at a water hole. Plains zebras have to drink regularly.

Grevy's zebras do not live in family groups like other zebras. The male zebras live alone on a large **territory** that covers ⅘ to 4 square miles (2 to 10 square kilometers). Each zebra marks the outside of his space with large piles of dung. These piles act as a warning to tell other Grevy's stallions to stay away.

In the breeding season the male tries to persuade a female zebra to come into his territory so he can mate with her. He chases off any other male that tries to enter his patch. Young Grevy's males live together in bachelor groups until they are old enough to break away and claim their own territory.

Grevy's zebras live alone. When two males meet, they may fight with one another.

Why Do Zebras Have Stripes?

Zebras are most famous for their stripes. But no one really knows what the stripes are for! Many animals have coats that are designed to **camouflage** them or hide them by blending into the background. But nothing could stand out more clearly on the grassy African plain than the zebra's black and white stripes!

Scientists do not know why zebras have stripes, but they have come up with a few ideas. One idea is that the stripes become a blur when the zebras run. Another idea is that the stripes may act as camouflage by blending into the shimmering heat haze on the plain. Perhaps the stripes confuse **predators** so that they find it hard to pick out one

Some people think that zebra stripes become a blur when the animals run. This would make it hard for a chasing lion or hyena to pick out one zebra from the herd.

individual from the herd. Another idea is that the stripes stop flies and mosquitoes from biting the zebras. Zebras love to groom one another. The stripes may be a way of showing other zebras the best patches to nibble and scratch.

Just like human fingerprints, all zebras have a slightly different pattern, most easily seen on their backsides. So perhaps the stripes help the zebras recognize each other. This would be important when the zebras are lining up to move off and need to find their right place in the line.

The different kinds of zebras have different types of stripes. Plains zebras have wide stripes. The pattern continues down the animal's legs and under its belly. Mountain zebras have narrow stripes on their shoulders. The stripes grow wider toward the back and the belly is white. Grevy's zebras have thin stripes that are very close together. These zebras also have a white belly.

Zebra stripes may look the same to us, but each animal has its own pattern.

13

Feeding

Zebras are **herbivores**, which means they do not eat meat, only plants. They live mainly on grass, but the mountain zebra will eat leaves and shoots as well.

Can you imagine eating for 18 hours a day? This is just what a zebra has to do to survive. Zebras have a much simpler digestive system than other grass-eating animals. They find it hard to get as much nutrition from their food so they have to keep grazing in order to get enough to eat. However, a zebra can eat tougher grass than most of the other grazers on the **savannas**.

Zebras have strong incisors (front teeth) that can bite off tall, tough grasses as well as short ones. Their back teeth

Zebras have soft, sensitive lips. They wrap their lips around long grass stalks to hold the grass as the incisors cut it.

are large and flat. These teeth are used for grinding. Their jaw muscles are very strong, which makes the zebras good at chewing the tough food.

Zebras are often the first animals to move into a patch of long grass. They nibble the long stalks with their sharp teeth. Zebras crop the grass so short they are sometimes called the lawnmowers of the savannas. When the zebras have cut the grass, other grazers can move in and eat it.

When food is scarce, and in times of drought, zebras may resort to nibbling the bark off trees. They can even dig up roots with their hoofs.

This zebra has found a tasty termite mound to lick. The termite mound provides minerals that the zebra cannot get from grass.

Zebras love to nibble and scratch one another. This shows that the zebras are friendly.

Getting Along

Zebras communicate with each other by smelling, touching, calling, and with body language. One way of getting to know one another is by **mutual grooming**.

Two zebras that are friendly toward each other will start mutual grooming by sniffing and nibbling the other's shoulders and neck. Then they stand next to each other, nose-to-tail, and groom each other's back. Sometimes the zebras just touch and rub heads instead of nibbling.

Mutual grooming often takes place between a mother and her foal and between zebras of the same mother. All the members of a family group will groom each other at some time. Mutual grooming plays a big part in bonding the family group together.

Another friendly practice is standing in pairs, nose-to-tail. The two zebras may rest their heads on each other's back. In this position they can swish flies off each other's head and shoulder with their tails. They can also see in all directions so they can look out for predators.

Young male zebras jostle each other in a friendly way. They also rub their faces together. Very young zebras nibble at their mother's legs or the legs of other young. The foals pretend to fight by biting at each other's legs.

Two zebras meeting for the first time or after a long separation go through a greetings ritual. First the zebras rub noses and sniff at each other. Then they rub cheeks and gradually move alongside each other until they reach the

When they are content or relaxed or comfortable with each other, two zebras stand nose-to-tail. Each zebra rests its head on the other zebra's back.

other's back. If they are satisfied that the other zebra is friendly, they rub their shoulders together and rest their head on the other animal's side.

Zebras are not always peaceful and friendly. When a male zebra is roused or threatened, he can become very aggressive. He has a range of facial expressions and body language to show his mood. If a zebra bares his teeth, lays his ears back, and swishes his tail from side to side, you know he is very angry. If he puts his head down low and weaves it from side to side, this means he is about to attack. He is very likely to follow through by kicking out with his front or hind legs.

It is easy to tell when a zebra is angry. It puts its ears back and bares its teeth. This female is chasing away another zebra's foal.

Fights between stallions are usually over a young female who is ready to mate. The fight starts with biting and wrestling. The two stallions jostle each other and rear up on their hind legs. Then they circle round each other, looking for a chance to bite.

Sometimes, the fight gets more serious. The contestants rear up on their hind legs and kick each other with their forelegs or turn back to back and kick with their hind legs. In the end one zebra will give up and run away, leaving the female to the winner.

Zebras make lots of different noises. They give the alarm to approaching danger by making a loud snort or a quiet gasp. If a zebra is injured in a fight, it squeals with pain. Stallions also squeal as a greeting when they meet. When a family group is grazing happily, the zebras make a blowing sound through loose lips as a sign of contentment.

Zebras often pretend to fight when they are playing. But sometimes, the fight gets more serious. The two zebras rear up and kick at each other with their front legs.

A Zebra's Day

A family group of zebras spends the night sleeping on a **bedding ground**. One individual in the group stays awake and on guard while the others sleep. At dawn the zebras get up and set off to find a good patch of grazing land. They walk along the trail in single file. Sometimes they are joined by gnus going in the same direction.

When they reach their grazing land the zebras spread out and spend most of the day cropping the grass. They are always on the lookout for danger. If the zebras see, hear, or smell a lion or hyena, they gallop off to safer grounds.

On a peaceful day, a zebra may decide to take a dustbath. It does this by finding a good patch of dust and then rolling

This zebra is taking a dustbath. This is a good way to get rid of any annoying insects.

in it. This is good for getting rid of ticks and biting insects. Other zebras see what is going on and decide they would like to take a bath in that patch of dust, too. They line up patiently, waiting their turn.

Rubbing up against a suitable tree or rock is another popular pastime. This may relieve itches, or again it may get rid of insects. Zebras stand in line for their turn at any tree or rock being used this way.

From time to time, the zebras visit the water hole to drink. In the late afternoon the zebras start moving back in single file to the bedding ground. This is when most of the friendly activities take place, with play and mock fights. At dusk, the zebras lie down to sleep. If the daytime grazing has not been good, they may wake during the night for short periods of nighttime grazing.

A zebra's day usually involves a trip to a water hole. Even when they are drinking, the animals are looking out for enemies.

This zebra foal is having a rest. But young zebras can stand almost as soon as they are born.

Bringing Up Young

A female zebra usually has one foal each year. The mare mates for the first time when she is about two to three years old. The foal is born about a year after the mating. The mare gives birth lying on her belly or her side, and the stallion stands watch nearby. The newborn baby zebra weighs about 73 lb (33 kg) if it is male. Female foals are slightly smaller. They weigh about 68 lb (31 kg).

Zebra foals learn quickly. They can stand up by themselves after about 15 minutes and can walk after just

30 minutes. Young zebras can **suckle** for milk within an hour of birth. After a few hours, they can run with the herd.

The mothers are very protective. They will not allow any other zebras to get close to the baby for the first few days. During this time, a tight bond forms between mother and foal. This makes sure the foal recognizes its own mother and does not mix her up with other members of the group.

The foal suckles its mother for up to a year and stays with its mother for the first two to three years of its life. Since the mare has a foal each year, this means that she may have three foals of various ages with her.

Young zebras suckle for up to a year. Their mother's milk is a rich food supply.

Enemies

Lions, hyenas, cheetahs, wild dogs, crocodiles, and humans are the zebra's enemies. Zebras have several natural safeguards against surprise attack. Their eyes are set well back on either side of the head, giving them very good "all round" vision. Zebras also have a very keen sense of smell, which can alert them to danger. Their large, mobile ears can pick up very faint sounds.

Zebras often graze alongside gnus. Lions and hyenas prefer to prey on gnus as they are smaller and less powerful than zebras. While the enemy is attacking a gnu, the zebras can escape. Ostriches also share the zebras' grazing grounds. These tall birds have excellent vision. If they see a

A group of zebras and gnus running away from an enemy. The enemy may attack a gnu, giving the zebras a better chance of escaping.

predator coming near, they may hiss loudly and begin to run. This warns the zebras, so they too can run away.

When hyenas attack a group of zebras, they try to catch a young or weak animal. The other zebras huddle around the threatened member and they all escape together. Stallions can be surprisingly aggressive in defending their family. The stallions may turn on the attackers and can cause a good deal of damage with their legs and teeth.

One stallion managed to fight off five hyenas. He kicked out with his legs and hit one of the hyenas on its head. Then he caught another hyena between his teeth and threw it more than 20 feet (6 meters). The remaining hyenas ran and the victorious zebra went back to join his family.

These zebras are being chased by a cheetah. The cheetah is faster but it soon tires. If these zebras keep running, they may be able to escape.

Saving the Zebra

Grevy's zebra and the mountain zebra were both listed as endangered by the World Conservation Union (IUCN) in 1996. This means that the numbers for both these species had dropped by half during the previous 10 years.

Until the mid-1970s Grevy's zebra was hunted for its decorative skin. This was made into rugs and other items. In 1977 hunting in Kenya was banned, yet the numbers of Grevy's zebra continued to drop. No one really knows why this happened. Unfortunately zebras are not

These zebra skins have been hung up to dry. The trade in their skins has made zebras a target for many hunters.

popular with farmers, because they can trample down crops on their way to water holes. Many farmers have fenced off their water holes to stop zebras using them. Perhaps the zebras died because they could not find enough water to drink. Farmers also shot large numbers of zebras because the zebras competed with cattle for grazing land.

Grevy's zebra has now disappeared completely in Somalia and is found only in south Ethiopia and Kenya. In the 1980s there were thought to be about 1,500 in Ethiopia and about 4,000 in Kenya, But these numbers are dropping fast. There are now only several thousand left in northern Kenya. In 1973, lots of countries got together to try and

Most of the endangered zebras now live on game reserves. They are a great attraction for tourists.

protect endangered animals. They all agreed not to trade in endangered species without special permits or sell items made from endangered species. This agreement is called the Convention on International Trade in Endangered Species (CITES). Grevy's zebra was listed in the agreement. Because of this, trade in the animal has virtually stopped. It is now hoped that the population in the Buffalo Springs nature **reserve** in Kenya and in other protected areas will increase. An action plan devised by the World Conservation Union in 1997 may also help to save Grevy's zebra.

The mountain zebra is also disappearing. There are only about 600 Cape mountain zebras left. Most of these live in protected areas such as the Mountain Zebra National Park in Cape Province. There are about 7,000 Hartmann's zebras

These Grevy's zebras live on the Samburu Game Reserve in Kenya.

left, most of them in protected areas in Namibia. In the middle of the 20th century there were about 50,000 to 70,000 of these animals, Many have been killed by farmers or by drought. Other mountain zebras have died because farm animals are eating the same food that the zebras eat. A **conservation** plan has been set up to look after mountain zebra species. This aims to increase the numbers of both the Cape mountain zebra and the Hartmann's zebra subspecies.

Nearly all the endangered zebras live in the game reserves and national parks of East and South Africa. If the conservation efforts now being made are successful, the numbers of zebras may start to increase. Herds of these beautiful striped creatures will continue to graze the great plains of Africa for many years to come.

This large zebra herd is grazing peacefully in a protected area of Africa.

Useful Addresses

For more information about zebras and how you can help protect them, contact these organizations:

Conservation International
1015 18th Street NW
Suite 1000
Washington, D.C. 20036

Defenders of Wildlife
1101 14th Street NW
Suite 1400
Washington, D.C. 20005

The Wildlife Conservation Society
2300 Southern Blvd.
Bronx, N.Y. 10480

Wildlife Preservation Trust International
1520 Locust Street
Suite 704
Philadelphia, PA 19104

World Wildlife Fund
1250 24th Street NW
Washington, D.C. 20037

World Wildlife Fund Canada
90 Eglinton Avenue East
Suite 504
Toronto
Ontario M4P 2Z7

Further Reading

Endangered Wildlife of the World (New York: Marshall Cavendish Corporation, 1994)

Saving Endangered Mammals Thane Maynard (New York: Franklin Watts, 1992)

The Zebra Carl Green and William Stafford (Mankato: Crestwood House, 1988)

Glossary

Bachelor group: A group of young male zebras that live together.

Bedding ground: A safe area chosen by a zebra family group to spend the night.

Camouflage: Color or patterns on an animal's skin that help it to blend into the background. This helps the animal hide from its enemies.

Conservation (Kon-ser-VAY-shun): Protecting the Earth's natural resources, such as plants, animals, and land.

Extinct (Ex-TINKT): No longer living anywhere in the world.

Foal: A young zebra.

Forage: Food.

Harem: The name given to a family of zebras.

Herbivore: An animal that only eats plants.

Mare: A female zebra.

Mate: When a male and female get together to produce young.

Mutual grooming: To search another animal's coat and remove any insects, dirt, or knots of fur. Zebras groom each other to show they are friendly.

Predator: A kind of animal that hunts and kills other animals.

Reserve: Land that has been set aside for plants and animals to live in without being harmed.

Savanna: A wide open plain. The main plant is grass, and there are very few trees.

Species: A kind of animal or plant. For example, Grevy's zebra is a species of zebra.

Stallion: A male zebra.

Subspecies: Plants or animals from the same species that are slightly different. Cape mountain zebras and Hartmann's zebras are subspecies of the Mountain zebra species.

Suckle: Feed on milk. Young zebras suckle their mothers.

Territory: The piece of land in which an animal lives. Some animals defend their territory from other animals.

Index